The Break of Day

by Hillary A. Hinds

The Break of Day

Written by Hillary A. Hinds

Copyright© 2021 by Hillary A. Hinds

All Scripture quotations are taken from the Holy Bible, King James Version, which is in the public domain.
The views expressed are those of the author alone.

ISBN: 978-1-7771012-7-5
Written by Hillary A. Hinds, Books4dNations Learning Innovations.
Book Cover Illustrations by StallionStudio88
Cataloguing in Publication may be obtained through Library and Archives Canada.

To the Nations' Kids
Love

Hillary

About the Book

The sounds you may hear at daybreak.

At the break of day, in the
stillness of the morning, the
sound you hear varies from the
birds' chirping, the crowing
rooster in the distance, the
cracking of tree branches as they
sway in the morning breeze. All
make the break of day something to
look forward to.

The Owl said his final hoot

as he greeted the morning

before he closes his eyes

to sleep.

"And a big *Cock a Doodle Doo* to you too!" said the big red rooster as he lifted his head while ruffling his feathers to greet the morning sun.

The lizard makes one last flip as
he crawls upon the log. "To you!"
he said as he stuck his tongue
out to clap at the fly who hissed
passed him.

ROAR

The lion rushes to the edge of
the cliff. He ROARS as he
greeted the burst of the sun
piercing through the clouds.

The monkey squeaks as he
greeted the morning. He
swings from a branch and
grabs a banana from a banana
tree nearby.

HOWL
HOWL

The wolf howls as the
morning sun pierced through
the thickets of the forest
trees. He glanced at the sun
before he disappeared in the
woods.

"Meow! Meow!" said the cat as she lifted her head to look at the sunbeam shining through the window before she snuggles up beside the foot of the bed.

"Snap!" The tree lifts the top

its branches and stretched out

wide as it greets the sunrise.

He[has]made everything beautiful in his

time, Ecclesiastes 3: 11

KJV.

About the Author

Hillary A Hinds is the author of the children's books *Rabbit Goes to Church*, *Blessings from Above*, *Mama Bear Knows Best* and *It's My Time* inspirational journal. She was born in Jamaica and currently resides in Canada. Hillary is the founder of Books4NAtionsKids of Saskatchewan, which provides faith-based books to kids and to different charities worldwide.